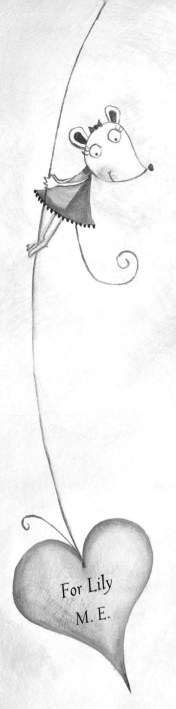

First published 2008 by Walker Books Ltd
87 Vauxhall Walk, London SE11 5HJ

1 3 5 7 9 10 8 6 4 2

Text © 2008 Max Eilenberg
Illustrations © 2008 Niamh Sharkey

This book has been typeset in Truesdell.

Printed in Singapore.

British Library Cataloguing in Publication Data:
a catalogue record for this book is available from
the British Library.

ISBN 978-1-4063-0798-6

www.walkerbooks.co.uk
www.niamhsharkey.com

For Lily
M. E.

For Nora
N. S.

Cinderella

Retold by Max Eilenberg

Illustrated by

Niamh Sharkey

WALKER BOOKS
AND SUBSIDIARIES
LONDON • BOSTON • SYDNEY • AUCKLAND

ONCE UPON A TIME there lived a girl, whose mother – the best mother in the whole world – had died, and whose father had married again.

The wedding was barely over before his new wife revealed her true nature. She was snobbish, mean and foul-tempered. Ooh, she was horrid!

And she was especially horrid to the girl, whose beauty made her own two daughters look positively hideous. The stepmother couldn't stand it.

The girl's father never said a word.
He didn't seem to notice how unkind the
stepmother was, how she blamed the girl
for everything. It was as if he had fallen
completely under the woman's spell.

Poor girl!
Every day the
stepmother made
her work so hard:
cook, clean,
dust, sweep,
rub, scrub,
peel, polish,
from first thing in the
morning to last thing
at night, until her
arms ached and
her head spun.

The sisters didn't care.
They were as nasty as their mother.
They loved to watch the girl work.

Ooh, they loved it.

They lolled around.
They laughed at her.
They mocked her tattered rags.

Then at night they made her sleep
in the corner by the chimney,
among the cinders ...

and they called her
Cinderella.

Now, it happened one day that the king decided to hold a great ball for his son, the prince. The stepmother made sure that her daughters were invited.

Invitation to a Ball
Friday 8 p.m.

The two sisters spent the whole week shopping. They bought expensive outfits, 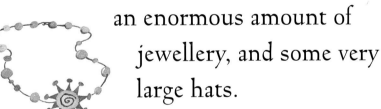 an enormous amount of jewellery, and some very large hats.

They thought they looked beautiful!
(In fact, they looked frightful.)

At last it was the day of the ball.
"I wish I could go," said Cinderella,
who had worked so hard to get the sisters ready.
"Well, you can't!" shouted the stepmother.
"No one cares about you! Get your mop out."
And off she went, with her husband trailing
silently behind her.
What a horrible woman!

Poor Cinderella was left all alone.
"I wish I could go to the ball," she sighed.
"And so you shall," said a pleasant voice.

Cinderella jumped in surprise.

There was a small, kindly looking woman,
hovering in the air beside her and holding
a large silver wand!

"Who are you?" gasped Cinderella.
"I'm your Fairy Godmother, dear.
Now, bring me a pumpkin
from the garden."

Cinderella had no idea how a pumpkin could help. But her Fairy Godmother simply tapped it with her wand.

Tap *tap* WHOOSH!!!

There stood a magnificent golden carriage. "Oh!" said Cinderella.

"Horses next," said the
Fairy Godmother. "We'll need some mice."

Tap *tap* went the wand. WHISH!!!

The mice turned into a splendid set of
horses, all a lovely dappled grey with a
distinguished hint of mouse colour.

"Now for a coachman," said the Fairy Godmother, pointing to the rat-trap. Inside were three fine rats. Cinderella chose the one with the longest whiskers.

KAPOUFF!!!

What a very proud coachman he was – and, my, what a superior moustache!

"Footmen," said the
Fairy Godmother.
"Lizards, please."

KAPAFFF!!!

Two tall footmen
climbed up behind the
carriage in their smart
tailcoats and their silken top
hats, as if they'd been born to
do nothing else in all their lives.

23

"That," said the Fairy Godmother,
"just leaves those rags."
Light sparkled from her wand.
Cinderella blinked. Her rags were gone.
In their place was a beautiful blue silk dress.
And there were pearls on her shoes ...
and sapphires in her hair! She could hardly
believe her eyes.
"Have a lovely time at the ball," said the
Fairy Godmother, "but do not stay past
midnight or all your magic will be lost."

"I promise!" said Cinderella.
And off she went.

At the palace, the ball had already begun, and music and laughter filled the air.

But when Cinderella arrived, everyone stopped.

She was so beautiful!

Nobody knew who she was, not even her sisters. The prince came to greet her, thinking she must be a grand princess. He asked her to dance. He asked her again ... and again!

Cinderella could not have been happier. But she remembered her promise and, at a quarter to midnight, slipped quietly away.

When the prince found she was gone,
he was miserable. He asked everyone her
name – but nobody knew who she was.

The very next morning, the king
announced that there would be
another ball, for his son longed to
see the beautiful princess again.

The two sisters spent the whole week
taking dancing lessons.
(They were useless.)
They spent a fortune on blue silk dresses.
(They still looked frightful.)

At last it was the day of the ball.

"I wish I could go," said Cinderella,
who had dreamed every night
of the handsome prince.

"Shut up!" shouted the
stepmother. "Get back to
your work." And off they
all went, slamming the
door behind them.

Cinderella sighed.

"Maybe I can help, dear," said a familiar voice.

It was the Fairy Godmother!

She waved her wand. The pumpkin carriage and its horses appeared, with the coachman and footmen all aboard.

Then suddenly Cinderella's rags were gone and she was wearing a dress of shimmering silver. Her shoes and her hair sparkled with diamonds. She could never have imagined anything so lovely.

The Fairy Godmother smiled. "Your carriage awaits," she said. "But remember to be home before midnight."

"I promise," said Cinderella happily.

At the palace, Cinderella outshone everyone. All the fine ladies wore blue, but her silver dress made them look quite ordinary.

The prince's heart leapt as he ran to take her hand. She was even lovelier than he remembered.

Then he led her to the dance floor.

How beautifully they danced together! Cinderella was so lost in happiness that she almost forgot the time. It was very nearly midnight before she remembered her promise, and quietly slipped away.

The prince ran out after her, but she was already gone and he returned to the palace full of longing, for she had stolen his heart.

The following morning, the king announced that there would be another ball that very night, for his son was too much in love to wait any longer.

The sisters shopped hastily for silver
dresses and diamonds. Cinderella worked
harder than ever to make them look
beautiful. (It simply wasn't possible.)

Then at last it was time to go.
"I wish—" said Cinderella.
"Well, don't!" shouted the stepmother.
And off they all went, slamming the
door behind them.

Poor Cinderella – how she longed to see
her prince!

"Don't worry, dear," said the kindly voice.
There was the Fairy Godmother again!
She waved her wand. The pumpkin
carriage and its horses appeared, with the
coachman and footmen standing ready.

Then Cinderella's rags were gone. Instead
she wore a gown of pure, bright gold.
And on her feet were slippers made of
glass – the finest, most magical shoes in
the whole wide world.

"Perfect," smiled the Fairy Godmother.
"Now don't forget to be back
        before midnight."
                "I promise," said Cinderella.

At the palace, Cinderella dazzled everyone. All the fine ladies wore silver now, but her golden dress made them look dull.

The prince was more in love than ever. He took her hand and they danced. They danced the whole evening, blissfully happy. Time melted away.

Cinderella didn't notice the hours passing – until suddenly BOING the clock started striking midnight.

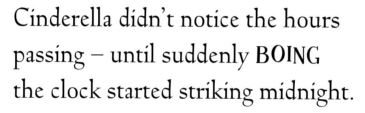

BOING

BOING BOING

BOING BOING

OH NO!!!

RUN, CINDERELLA, RUN!
RUN, RUN, RUN!

She ran so fast her shoe fell off.
There was no time to pick it up.

BOINGGG!!!!

The prince ran out after her, but
she was gone. All that remained
was a precious glass slipper.

The next morning the prince announced that he would marry the girl whose foot fitted the slipper.

Then he set out to find her.

He travelled the kingdom and stopped at every house.

Every girl he met tried the slipper on,
for every girl wanted to marry the prince.

But the slipper fitted none of them,
and the prince had to keep on looking.

At last he came to the stepmother's house. "Meet my daughters," she said, rubbing her hands with glee.

Well, how the sisters tried.
They pinched and pushed, they
squeezed and shoved – but they
couldn't make the slipper fit.
The stepmother was furious.
"Is there no one else?"
sighed the prince.
"No, there isn't," she snapped.

"Yes, there IS," said a voice Cinderella had
almost forgotten. Surely it couldn't be?
She hardly dared believe it…

Her father!
It was as if he had woken from
a deep sleep. He turned towards
her and smiled. "There's my
daughter," he said.

Cinderella stepped forward from
the shadows, her heart beating.
"May I try the slipper?" she asked.

The prince looked closely at her
face. Then, carefully, gently, he
knelt down and held out the
glass slipper.

It fitted perfectly!

"It's you!" cried the prince, taking Cinderella in his arms and kissing her. "You are my love!"
"At last!" said another voice. It was the Fairy Godmother. She waved her wand and once more Cinderella's rags were transformed.

Very soon afterwards Cinderella and the prince were married. Cinderella's father threw the confetti, and the king led the cheers. The stepmother and the sisters did their best to look pleased. (They didn't quite manage it.)

As for Cinderella, her wishes had all come true. She loved her prince and her prince loved her. And that's the way it was,

happily ever after.